TABLE OF CONTENTS

Olaf mails a letter

"Olaf," said his mother, "will you mail a letter for me?"

"What will you give me?" Olaf asked.

"Nothing," said his mother. "You should do it because I ask."

"O.K.," said Olaf.

careful!

Candy
Store

School

start

Go

Easy

"I will give you a cookie when you get back," said his mother.

"For mailing the letter?" Olaf said.

"No! Because I want you to have a cookie," said his mother.

14

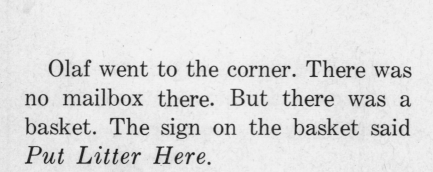

Main Street

BOOKS

STOP

wait!

GO

NO TURNS

grocery

PU
LIT
I-

Olaf went to the corner. There was
no mailbox there. But there was a
basket. The sign on the basket said
Put Litter Here.

"I can read," said Olaf. "But they can't spell." He put the letter in the basket.

Olaf ran home and told his mother. "Oh, no, Olaf!" she said. "A litter basket is to throw things away in."

"Oh," said Olaf. "Why didn't the sign say so?"

"It did," said his mother. "Now get the letter and mail it. Eat this cookie on the way."

"O.K.," said Olaf.

There was a truck by the basket. A man was throwing the papers in the truck.

"Stop!" said Olaf.

It was too late. Olaf told the man about the letter.

"I'll help you look," said the man. They looked for the letter.

Some of the papers blew away. Olaf ran after them.

"Here it is!" Olaf said. "Thank you
for helping me."
"Glad to help," said the man.

Olaf put the letter in the mailbox. He said, "Why don't they tell us all the words at the same time? Then things like this can't happen."

Olaf pulls

It was not time for school. But it was too cold to be out. The children went in.

"Look at that sign," said Olaf. "It says *Pull*. Help me."

"Do you think we should?" said Cathy.

"It says *Pull*," said Olaf.

The children got their books. They put them on the floor. Olaf got on the books. The sign was still too high. He saw Mr. Snaps walking by.

"We need a box, please," said Olaf.

"I'm busy," said Mr. Snaps. "But I will find you a box."

Mr. Snaps came back with a box. "Now I have work to do," he said.

Olaf put the box under the sign. He got on the box. And he pulled.

Just then the fire bell rang.

Olaf's teacher ran down the hall.
"Get in line," Miss Twist said. They
all got in line.

"March," said Miss Twist. The children marched out of school and down the street.

"Stop!" said Miss Twist. "I didn't say you could march home."

Soon fire trucks came. Policemen came. Everyone who lived near by came.

The firemen went in the school. They were gone a long time. Then they came out.

"There is no fire," said a fireman.

"Who pulled the fire bell?" asked a policeman.

"Pull?" said Olaf.

"Did you do it?" said the policeman.

"But it said *Pull*," said Olaf. "Are you going to put me in jail?"

"No, but I will scold you," said the policeman. "It is good to read. But you must think, too. Read and think."

"Yes," said Olaf.

A fireman said, "You must not pull something that says *Pull* if you don't know what it is."

"I'm sorry," said Olaf. "I won't do it again."

"Anyway," said Miss Twist, "we had to have a fire drill soon." The policeman and fireman laughed.

"And it was fun to see," said Olaf. "More fun than school."

"Olaf!" said Miss Twist.

"Didn't you have fun?" Olaf asked.

"Well, never mind," said Miss Twist. "March back to school."

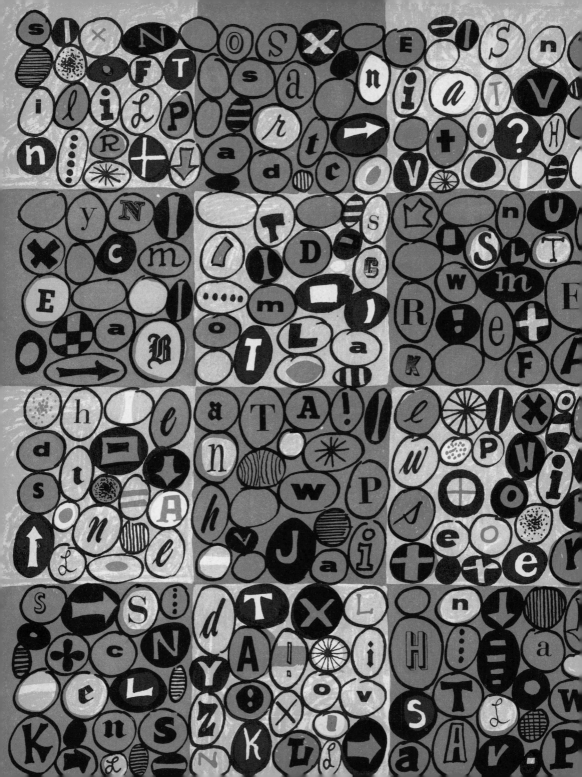

Olaf goes to the library

"Now you can read a little," Miss Twist said. "So we can go to the library. You may each take one book." The children got in line and marched down the hall.

Olaf took a book off the shelf. "Hey,
I can read this!" he yelled. "I'll read
it to you."

"Shh!" said Miss Twist.

"Shh!" said the library lady.

"Shh!" said all the children.

Olaf saw another book he wanted. And another. And another. He tried to hold all the books. They wiggled and shook.

"Where is Olaf?" said Miss Twist.

CRASH! All the books fell down.

"Oh, there you are," she said. "I should have known. What are you going to do with all those books, Olaf?"

"Read them?" asked Olaf.

"I said one book," said Miss Twist.
"But you are a good reader. You may
take two books."

"Which two?" Olaf asked.

"Close your eyes and take two,"
Miss Twist said.

"O.K.," said Olaf.

"And do you see that sign? What does it say?" Miss Twist asked.

"I don't know," Olaf said. "You told me to close my eyes."

"Well, open them," said Miss Twist.

"Sure," said Olaf.

"Say *surely*," said Miss Twist.

"You want me to call you Shirley?" Olaf asked.

"Never mind," said Miss Twist. "Read the sign."

"It says quit," said Olaf.
"No," said Miss Twist.
"Quite?" Olaf asked.

"I'll help you," Miss Twist said.
She looked at the sign and said, "Shh!"

"Don't you want me to tell you?"
Olaf whispered.

"Read the sign," Miss Twist said.
"Oh, it says QUIET!" Olaf yelled.

"Shh," said Miss Twist.
"Shh," said the library lady.
"Shh," said all the children.

Miss Twist walked away. She
looked back at Olaf. "Remember the
sign," she said.

She did not see Mr. Snaps and his
pail of water. "Do not yell," said
Miss Twist.

Olaf whispered, "Look out!"

"Do not—" she said.

SPLASH! She walked right into the pail.

"I tried to tell you," Olaf said.

"I know," said Miss Twist.

"Well, anyway," Olaf said, "I'll remember how to read QUIET."

Olaf ran home with his books.
"Mother, come here!" he yelled.

"What is it?" asked his mother.

"You don't have to read to me any
more," said Olaf. "Now I'll read to
you!"

The End

Special Notice to Book Club Members

★ This book is a selection of the WEEKLY READER CHILDREN'S BOOK CLUB. It was chosen especially for our members by the Weekly Reader Selection Board after careful consideration of hundreds of other books for girls and boys.

Members of the WEEKLY READER CHILDREN'S BOOK CLUB receive six or more exciting books during the year — including one or more Free Bonus Books upon joining. They also receive a Membership Certificate, Club Bookmarks and regular Book Club Bulletins.

We hope you enjoy this book. Your friends will enjoy it, too. If they are not already members, why not ask them to join the WEEKLY READER CHILDREN'S BOOK CLUB.

WEEKLY READER
Children's Book Club
Education Center • Columbus 16, Ohio